CHERYL HARNESS

GHOSTS

OF THE

20TH

CENTURY

SIMON & SCHUSTER BOOKS FOR YOUNG READERS

SIMON & SCHUSTER BOOKS FOR YOUNG READERS
An imprint of Simon & Schuster Children's Publishing Division
1230 Avenue of the Americas, New York, New York 10020
Copyright © 2000 by Cheryl Harness
SIMON & SCHUSTER BOOKS FOR YOUNG READERS is an imprint of Simon & Schuster.
Book design by Paul Zakris
The text of this book is set in 12-point Impress.
The illustrations are rendered in watercolor, ink, and colored pencil on Strathmore illustration board.
Printed in Hong Kong
10 9 8 7 6 5 4 3 2 1
Library of Congress Cataloging-in-Publication Data
Harness, Cheryl.
Ghosts of the twentieth century / by Cheryl Harness.—1st ed.
p.   cm.
Summary: While on a field trip to a museum, a young boy encounters Albert Einstein, who gives him a whirlwind tour of the twentieth century.
ISBN 0-689-82118-2
1. Twentieth century-Miscellanea—Juvenile literature. 2. History, Modern—20th century-Miscellanea—Juvenile literature. [1. Twentieth century—Miscellanea. 2. History, Modern—20th century—Miscellanea.] I. Title.
CB426.H35 2000
909.82—dc21
98-38103

The twentieth century looms before us big with the fate of many nations.
—*Theodore Roosevelt, April 10, 1899*

Author's Note

The twenty-first century begins, if one is going to be official about it, at 12:01 A.M. January 1, 2001. It is proper to look back at the past one hundred years: the maps with many changes, dates and places, and news bulletins that echo down through the years: TITANIC SINKS! WAR! ARMISTICE! WALL STREET CRASHES! PEARL HARBOR ATTACKED! VICTORY! BERLIN WALL TUMBLES DOWN.

How do I, in one slim book, clearly tell about something as messy as millions of people getting born, living their lives, thinking up wonderful or horrible ideas over the course of one hundred years? Perhaps I can give you a taste of what it was like and what was on people's minds during the past ten decades, and how the present came to be. We're surrounded by the outcomes of decisions made by everyone who's lived in this twentieth century—and before. It's as if they haunt us. And we're right along with them, affecting the twenty-first century—and beyond!

me of smoking factories, skyscrapers, mighty ocean liners and battleships, colonial empires, electricity and automobiles.

— 1st U.S. OLYMPICS: 1904 —

GTIME becomes part of JAZZ music ❀ ESCALATOR is invented ❀ Commonwealth of AUSTRALIA is CREATED ❀ Oil drilling begins in PERSIA ❀ St.LOUIS WORLD's FAIR

1904
Work continues on the PANAMA CANAL.

JAMES BARRIE writes "Peter Pan"

1905

ALBERT EINSTEIN writes his revolutionary ideas about tiny particles of LIGHT, about TIME, MATTER and ENERGY: [1905-1915] $E = MC^2$

'St.Petersburg, Russia
"BLOODY SUNDAY" January 22, 1905
Unarmed strikers attacked at the CZAR's WINTER PALACE

April 18, 1906
EARTHQUAKE and FIRE leaves San Francisco in ruins and kills 700 people

ROALD AMUNDSEN of NORWAY explores the NORTHWEST PASSAGE, determines position of Magnetic NORTH POLE.

EUROPE before the GREAT WAR

Wilhelm II
Kaiser of
GERMANY

Nicholas II
Czar of
RUSSIA

George V
King of
BRITAIN

cousins!

Franz-Josef
Emperor of
AUSTRIA-HUNGARY

PRESIDENT
RAYMOND
POINCARÉ

the ALLIES

the CENTRAL
POWERS

the NEUTRAL
COUNTRIES

Neutral countries that
joined the CENTRAL POWERS
later on

Neutral countries
that later joined
the ALLIES
(such as the U.S.)

SCOTLAND

GREAT
BRITAIN

NORTH
SEA

DENMARK

IRELAND

WALES

LONDON

ATLANTIC
OCEAN

NETHERLAND

BELGIUM

BERLIN

EAST
PRUSSIA

GERMAN EMPIRE

POLAND

RUSSIAN EMPIRE

MOSCOW

PARIS

LUX.

LORRAINE

ALSACE

SWITZ.

EMPIRE
OF
AUSTRIA-HUNGARY

VIENNA

FRANCE

ITALY

It all began in
SARAJEVO

SERBIA

ROMANIA

BLACK SEA

PORTUGAL

SPAIN

MEDITERRANEAN SEA

CORSICA

SARDINIA

ROME

MONTENEGRO

ALBANIA

BULGARIA

GREECE

ATHENS

OTTOMAN EMPIRE
TURKEY

SICILY

Kings choosing up sides like jealous boys in the schoolyard!
Whipping up national pride to get millions of men to go to a
meaningless war! That's what made this horror, called "the
war to end all wars." Wishful thinking, my boy.

WWI : 1914~1918   A great chain of events is put in motion...

D.W. GRIFFITH makes a movie: "BIRTH OF A NATION" 1915 ◎ MARGARET SANGER opens the first birth control clinic : 1916

1917: After 3 years, 1,700,000
RUSSIAN soldiers killed,
5,000,000 wounded, 200,000
taken prisoner, RUSSIA
collapsed into REVOLUTION
led by Bolshevik NIKOLAI LENIN

GERMAN submarine warfare
leads President WILSON of the U.S.
to declare WAR on GERMANY
April 6, 1917

• WAR SONG "OVER THERE"
is written by GEORGE M. COHAN

July 17, 1918
Czar Nicholas II
and his family
are murdered
by the Bolsheviks

ARMISTICE:
• The fighting came to an end November 11, 1918
the 11th hour, the 11th day, the 11th month

Twenty
million
people
die
in a
worldwide
influenza
epidemic

June 28, 1919
GERMANY signs the PEACE TREATY
at the palace of VERSAILLES, FRANCE
The victorious ALLIES demanded
that the defeated, broke and hungry
GERMANS pay $32 billion in
"war damages". 26 million soldiers
and civilians were dead, EUROPE was
in tatters — and the seeds had
been planted for WORLD WAR Two.

THE GREAT DEPRESSION: Banks close, businesses fail, times are hard,

JAPAN invades MANCHURIA: 1931 ✦ Charles Lindbergh's baby boy is kidnapped and killed:1932 ✦ STARVATION in USSR

1930
The ninth planet, **PLUTO** is discovered by C.W. TOMBAUGH

GRANT WOOD paints "American Gothic"

1931
The Empire State Building is Completed

PEARL BUCK writes "The Good Earth"

1932 The DEPRESSION goes from bad to worse. More and more people are hungry and out of a job.

FRANKLIN DELANO **ROOSEVELT** promises a "NEW DEAL" and is elected President of the U.S.

LAURA INGALLS WILDER: "Little House in the Big Woods"

1933
ADOLF HITLER becomes Chancellor (prime minister) of GERMANY

FDR begins his radio "fireside chats"

MARX BROTHERS' film: "Duck Soup"

1934
The world's first surviving quintuplets, the DIONNE sisters, are born in CANADA

P.L. TRAVERS: "Mary Poppins"

FRANK CAPRA film: "It Happened One Night"

SHIRLEY TEMPLE is the most popular child-star of the early 1930s

In the course of this war, the worst ever, nearly 55 million people died and many more suffered in EUROPE, RUSSIA and AFRICA, on the seas, and finally and horribly, in JAPAN. Atomic bombs were dropped. These bombs were made possible when I showed that the splitting of an atom could release tremendous energy. These terrible bombs ended the war - but now humans knew that they could destroy themselves once and for all.

UNION OF SOVIET SOCIALIST REPUBLICS

AFGHANISTAN

TIBET
NEPAL
INDIA

CHINA 1938
The people of NANKING were treated with terrible brutality

MANCHURIA 1931

KOREA

Emperor HIROHITO
The Emperor remained silent as his military leaders took over eastern CHINA and the nations and islands of southern ASIA and the PACIFIC OCEAN.

B-29 AIR RAIDS
JUNE 15, 1944-AUG 1945

TOKYO

NAGASAKI AUGUST 9
HIROSHIMA AUGUST 6, 1945

SHANGHAI

OKINAWA-APRIL 1-JUNE 21 1945
IWO JIMA FEB 19-MAR. 16, 1945

PACIFIC OCEAN

MIDWAY JUNE 4-6 1942

PEARL HARBOR DEC. 7 1941

BURMA 1942

LUZON OCT. 20, 1944 - FEB 6, 1945

BATAAN

FRENCH INDOCHINA 1941

THAILAND 1941

1942 LEYTE GULF OCT. 23-26, 1944

WAKE ISLAND Dec. 23, 1941

PHILIPPINES

PELELIU ISLAND SEPT. 15-OCT 13, 1944

Mariana Islands GUAM JULY 21-AUG 10 1944

JAPANESE EMPIRE by 1942

MALAYA 1942

BORNEO

NEW GUINEA

BATTLE of BISMARK MAR. 2-5 SEA 1943

TARAWA NOV. 20-23 1943

Gilbert Islands

JAVA SEA FEB 27, 1942

bitter fighting at GUADALCANAL "island of death"
Aug. 7, 1942 Feb. 8, 1943

CORAL SEA May 4-8, 1942

THE SECOND WORLD WAR, WWII: 1939~1945

F.D.R. is elected to a third term as president: 1940 ◊ ORSON WELLES' film: "Citizen Kane" ◊ MT. RUSHMORE opens: 1941

GERMAN bombing raids begin over blacked-out BRITAIN 1939

1940

BLITZKRIEG! 1941
(LIGHTNING WAR)
ADOLF HITLER'S GERMAN army invades NORWAY, DENMARK, HOLLAND, BELGIUM, FRANCE, and LUXEMBOURG

May 29-June 4
336,000 British soldiers, trapped between GERMAN tanks and the sea, are rescued from DUNKIRK, FRANCE

7:55 A.M. SUNDAY, DECEMBER 7 "a date which will live in infamy" FDR
JAPAN attacks the U.S. NAVAL base at PEARL HARBOR, HAWAII. The U.S. declared WAR

"JOLTIN' JOE" DiMAGGIO of the N.Y. YANKEES hits safely in 56 games.

1940: WALT DISNEY'S film: "FANTASIA"
MAUD HART LOVELACE: "Betsy-Tacy"
ERIC KNIGHT: "Lassie Come-Home"

GERMANY, ITALY and JAPAN join together in a pact.

ROBERT McCLOSKEY writes "Make Way for Ducklings"
H.A. REY writes "Curious George"

on JAPAN the next day. Then, GERMANY and ITALY declared WAR on the U.S.

and new fears—of Communism, and the **BOMB**—and new questions about the rights of BLACK AMERICANS—

1952 ⊕ Mr. & Mrs. Rosenberg, U.S. citizens, are executed as Communist SPIES : 1953 ⊕ Fidel Castro lands in Cuba : 1956

1955 ROSA PARKS refuses to give up her seat at the front of the bus: THE MONTGOMERY, ALABAMA BUS BOYCOTT —begins.—

1956 Reverend MARTIN LUTHER KING, JR. gains national fame as the leader of the struggle for civil rights—

ELVIS PRESLEY becomes a ROCK & ROLL LEGEND

• Oct. 3, 1955: television show "CAPTAIN KANGAROO"

1957 The USSR launches SPUTNIK: first artificial satellite

U.S. soldiers help black children go to school in LITTLE ROCK, ARK.

DR. SEUSS writes "Cat in the Hat"

1958 ALASKA becomes the **49TH** STATE

HULA HOOPS!

AMERICAN VAN CLIBURN wins the TCHAIKOVSKY INTERNATIONAL PIANO COMPETITION MOSCOW, USSR

1959 HAWAII becomes the **50TH** STATE in the UNION—

• The BARBIE doll is introduced
• BUDDY HOLLY (and the music) dies.

1963 BIRMINGHAM, ALABAMA

The Civil War and the Emancipation Proclamation weren't enough to free a people. Old fearful ways of thinking die hard. Here's some of the worst fighting in African Americans' long struggle for the civil rights to vote, to be educated, and to be treated with dignity as U.S. citizens.

The FRIENDSHIP 7 — The 1st U.S. ASTRONAUT to orbit the earth was JOHN GLENN

THE NEW FRONTIER: 1960~1964: The COLD WAR is colder, racial

1960: U.S. spy plane is shot down over U.S.S.R. ◎ The "TRITON" U.S. nuclear Submarine goes on the 1st round-the-world

1960
75 million Americans watched presidential candidates JOHN F. KENNEDY and RICHARD M. NIXON DEBATE on television

BUSES BOMBED! "FREEDOM RIDES" — to make sure Blacks could ride the interstate buses. PEOPLE are KILLED — black and white.

HARPER LEE writes "To Kill a Mockingbird"

1961
April 12: 1st manned space flight: RUSSIAN Cosmonaut: YURI A. GAGARIN

May 5: Alan B. Shepard is the 1st U.S. astronaut in space.

August 13: work is begun on a WALL to divide BERLIN, GERMANY to keep EAST BERLINERS (under Soviet control) from escaping to FREEDOM in the WEST

1962
The U.S. and the USSR almost go to nuclear WAR

NIKITA KHRUSHCHEV of U.S.S.R. puts missiles on the island of CUBA

— October 14-28 —
CUBAN MISSILE CRISIS

CHARLES M. SCHULZ: "Happiness is a Warm Puppy"
MADELEINE L'ENGLE: "A Wrinkle in Time"

WE WANT A WHITE SCHOOL

FEBRUARY 20, 1962 • 99 to 162.5 miles high • 3 orbits: 4 hours, 55 minutes.

struggle is hotter — and a young president is killed.

under water trip ⊙ 1963: VALENTINA TERESHKOVA of RUSSIA: 1ST female astronaut ⊙ People dance the TWIST, the FRUG, WATUSI, MASHED POTATO....

President KENNEDY insisted they be removed — or else.
They were.

MARILYN MONROE, actress, dies. Aug 5, 1962

1963 WASHINGTON D.C.
August 28: To 200,000 "FREEDOM MARCHERS" Dr. MARTIN LUTHER KING declares, "I have a dream...."

MAURICE SENDAK. "Where the Wild Things Are"

NOVEMBER 22. DALLAS, TEXAS PRESIDENT JOHN F. KENNEDY is shot and killed by LEE HARVEY OSWALD.

The FIRST LADY, Mrs. KENNEDY, and her children moved the nation with their courage

1964 The BEATLES, British musicians, come to AMERICA

GEORGE RINGO PAUL JOHN

• LYNDON JOHNSON is elected President
• In South Africa, anti-apartheid activist, NELSON MANDELA is sent to prison.

LOUISE FITZHUGH writes "Harriet the Spy"

THE SEVENTIES: 1972-1979 Equality for Women! Save the Planet!

1972: Five burglars are arrested at Democratic Headquarters at the WATERGATE complex ◉ militant Native Americans occupy

- **NIXON 1972** visits CHINA
- civil war breaks out in LEBANON
- Israeli OLYMPIC athletes killed by Arab terrorists

RICHARD ADAMS: "Watership Down"

U.S. ground troops and prisoners of war leave **VIETNAM in 1973**

Yom Kippur War in the Middle East: OIL is very expensive!!

1974 Girls are allowed into the LITTLE LEAGUE.

RICHARD NIXON becomes the 1st U.S. president to resign his office

WATERGATE: a covered-up series of illegal activities to re-elect the president ROCKS the U.S. Government.

APRIL 30, 1975 The VIETNAM WAR comes to an end. 58,000 Americans and many thousands more Vietnamese are dead.

1976 14-year-old gymnast NADIA COMANECI of ROMANIA WINS 3 OLYMPIC Gold medals

Thousands are dying in the killing fields of CAMBODIA

◉ U.S. VIKING unmanned spacecraft completes a 500 million mile journey to the planet MARS.

STEVEN SPIELBERG film: "JAWS"

ALEX HALEY writes "ROOTS" SYLVESTER STALLONE film: "ROCKY"

what is the world talking about? AIDS, international terrorism – and the IRON CURTAIN is coming down.

1985: MIKHAIL GORBACHEV comes to power in the U S S R ➤ 1986: ACCIDENT at nuclear power plant CHERNOBYL, U S S R

1985
- HALLEY'S Comet appears again.
- President RONALD REAGAN is sworn for a 2nd term in Office
- 73 years after she sank, the great ship **TITANIC** is found.

1986
IRAN·CONTRA SCANDAL
missiles·money·hostages in LEBANON·"contra" rebels in NICARAGUA: the U.S. government weaves a tangled web.

U.S. space shuttle "CHALLENGER" explodes killing seven astronauts, including CHRISTA McAULIFFE, a science teacher

RONALD REAGAN, U.S. President

1987
TERRY WAITE of BRITAIN joins the Americans and Europeans chained and blindfolded in the cellars of BEIRUT, LEBANON

1988
8 years of WAR between IRAQ and IRAN ends.

PAN AM 103: a jet full of 258 people is blown up over LOCKERBIE, SCOTLAND, Dec. 21

1989
- F.W. de KLERK of SOUTH AFRICA begins reforms that will end APARTHEID

June 9 Hundreds of Chinese students wanting democracy & freedom of speech are killed in TIANANMEN SQUARE, BEIJING, CHINA

Communist government in ROMANIA comes to an end Dec. 31

PAUL FLEISCHMAN: "Joyful Noise"

I have to write a science report. I don't know whether to do the Pathfinder going to Mars, or those guys who cloned sheep. What do you think?

* * *

Do the clone thing. That's so science fiction. Wouldn't it be cool if they could make a copy of Jordan? Then both of us could go out with him!

* * *

I won't be going anywhere until my mom gets a new job. I have to baby-sit L.T. (short for "Little Terror").

* * *

That stinks, for you and your mom. She was at that company for a long time and they let her go, just like that.

* * *

Somebody in another country where people don't get paid very much will do her job. Scary, isn't it?

THE NINETIES: 1990~1999 · WORLD POPULATION: 5.3 billion and growing

1990: NELSON MANDELA is released from prison in SOUTH AFRICA ◯ A divided GERMANY is reunited ◯ 1991: western

The HUBBLE space telescope is launched into orbit, 370 miles above the earth.

1990

free elections in ROMANIA for the 1ST time in 53 years.

· JIM HENSON, creator of the MUPPETS, passes away

· film: "HOME ALONE"

January 16, 1991 SADDAM HUSSEIN of IRAQ invaded KUWAIT ~ DESERT STORM WAR begins.

IRAN IRAQ SAUDI ARABIA KUWAIT PERSIAN GULF

The U.S. and a host of nations liberate KUWAIT: February 27.

The nations of the Balkans became YUGOSLAVIA in 1918.

SLOVENIA CROATIA BOSNIA-HERZEGOVINA SARAJEVO SERBIA MONTENEGRO KOSOVO ALBANIA MACEDONIA GREECE

In 1991, when the communist government fell apart WAR began among the people. At least 200,000 die, more are hurt, or forced from their homes as refugees.

The SOVIET UNION falls apart

BORIS YELTSIN declares RUSSIAN independence August 31

1992 Terrible race riots in LOS ANGELES after four white policemen who beat up a black man are found "not guilty"

1993 BILL CLINTON is inaugurated as the 42nd president

YITZHAK RABIN of ISRAEL and YASSIR ARAFAT (PLO) make peace

DENISE FLEMING: "In the Small Small Pond"

On televisions, on computer screens: never have the people of the world had such an opportunity to know each other.

hostages are released from BEIRUT, LEBANON ⊕ 1994: Americans focus on the trial of O.J. SIMPSON ⊕ 1995: EARTHQUAKE: KOBE, JAPAN

1994
Fighting between the HUTU & the TUTSI peoples: thousands die in RWANDA.

Former political prisoner NELSON MANDELA becomes the first black president of SOUTH AFRICA.

April 19 1995
The federal office building in OKLAHOMA CITY is bombed by an American.

1996
Scientists in SCOTLAND CLONED two sheep

• A jet full of 228 people explodes just after taking off from NEW YORK.

• MADELEINE ALBRIGHT: 1st woman U.S. SECRETARY of STATE.

August 31, 1997
PRINCESS DIANA GREAT of BRITAIN is killed.

MOTHER TERESA of Calcutta, India dies.

FRANK McCOURT: "Angela's Ashes"
DAVID WISNIEWSKI: "GOLEM"

1998
• FLOODS in CHINA (millions homeless)
• BOMBS in AFRICA
• WAR in YUGOSLAVIA (refugees suffer)
SCANDAL in the WHITE HOUSE

BILL CLINTON U.S. President

December 31, midnight 1999
Billions of EARTHLINGS celebrate the end of the 20TH CENTURY.

Glossary

Allies: Countries that agree to help each other and fight on the same side if there's war.

Apartheid: South Africa's official policy meant to keep people of color apart from the white population. It was officially ended by F. W. de Klerk and Nelson Mandela in 1994.

Baby Boomers: The huge generation of children born between the years 1946 and 1962, when soldiers in World War II came home, got married, and made families.

Beatnik: A mid-1950s rebel against mainstream American culture, an admirer of poetry and jazz.

Berlin Wall: The most powerful symbol of the **Cold War** between the USSR and the West (the capitalist countries of Europe and North America). Between 1961 and 1989, at least 77 people were killed trying to escape to freedom. It was only one part of the imaginary **Iron Curtain** that separated people under **Communist** control from the rest of the world.

Bootlegger: During **Prohibition** (1920–1933), when selling alcohol was against the law, **bootleggers** sold liquor that had been sneaked into the United States. Sometimes people made alcoholic drinks at home to drink and/or sell. That's where we got the term **bathtub gin**.

Boycotting: When many people get together and refuse to use or buy something in order to get their idea across.

Capitalism: An economy in which individuals own farms and factories. Businesses compete with one another, doing business to make money.

Charleston: A fast, twisty dance popular in the 1920s.

Civil Rights: What citizens of a country ought to have: personal freedoms, the right to vote, and being treated equally.

Communism: A political party, a way of life, a **socialist** system in which the government owns and controls where people work. Socialists think that if factories and land are owned by everybody, instead of by individuals, then everybody might be treated more fairly. The leaders also wanted to control how people lived and thought. This idea got going in **Russia** in the Revolution of 1917. Russia and her neighbors became the **Union of Soviet Socialist Republics (USSR)**, also known as the **Soviet Union**. Because red's the color of the Soviet flag, Communists are called **Reds**, or just **Commies**. Americans were so upset that countries would fall, like dominoes, under the power of Communism that the United States went to war in **Korea** and in **Vietnam**. We fought a tense **Cold War**, and were afraid for many years of a big hot war with the USSR, with atomic weapons. In 1989 and 1990, Communism in Russia and Europe came to an end. It never quite worked.

Democracy: Where people vote to elect representatives in their government.

Flapper: What people called bold, flashy young women in the 1920s.

Hippie: Comes from the idea of being "hip" or knowing what's cool. So does **hip-hop**. In the 1960s, a hippie was a young person rejecting the grown-up, power-holding, suit-wearing, Vietnam War-making world, known as the **Establishment**.

Holocaust: The organized, on-purpose killing of 6 million European Jews, as well as Gypsies, homosexuals, and Communists, by the Nazis in and before World War II.

Jitterbugger: Someone who danced this fast, swingy dance in the 1940s.

Mah-jongg: This Chinese game, played with little tiles, was very popular in the 1920s. It was fashionable to wear a Japanese robe (**kimono**) while you played it.

Marshall Plan: In 1948, President Truman and his advisers devised a plan for America to help Europe get over World War II partly so the people there wouldn't be so homeless and hungry they'd be tempted to become Communists.

NRA (National Recovery Administration): It was started in 1933 as part of President Franklin Roosevelt's **New Deal** to turn economic conditions around. Nowadays, when people say "NRA" they mean National Rifle Association, and they're mostly talking about the right to carry guns.

Nobel Prize: Given every year to people who've worked for the "good of humanity" in medicine, literature, physics, economics, chemistry, or peace. This was the idea of Alfred Nobel, the Swedish inventor of dynamite.

Settlement House: A place in a city neighborhood that tries to help people live better.

Solidarity: The Polish **labor union** led by Lech Walesa to improve pay and working conditions. The union's actions in the early 1980s led to expanded civil rights and, ultimately, the downfall of Poland's strict Communist government.

Suffragette: Someone who worked and fought for the right of women to vote.

Tiananmen Square, Beijing: The last years of the 20th century have brought greater economic freedom to Communist China. But students who'd gathered in the great square by the Gate of Heavenly Peace (Tian An Men) to demonstrate for democracy and civil rights were crushed by their government on June 4, 1989.

Verdun: A town in France where so much fighting happened for so long that it became a symbol for how stuck, hopeless, and bloody the First World War was.

Wobbly: A member of the **IWW** (Industrial Workers of the World) union, started in 1905.

Yuppie: Young Urban Professional. A busy, full-of-themselves, hardworking, big-spending, **Me-generation** thing in the 1980s.

Ziegfeld girl: A pretty girl who sang and danced in shows, called "Ziegfeld Follies," in theaters. They were put together by Florenz Ziegfeld, and were very popular in the first part of the 20th century.

Zionism: A political movement for a Jewish homeland in Palestine.

20TH CENTURY PEOPLE

MARY McLEOD BETHUNE (1875-1955)

Mrs. Bethune gave her life to bringing better education to black Americans. An adviser to Presidents Hoover, F. D. Roosevelt, and Truman, she was the first black woman to head a federal government agency.

GEORGE WASHINGTON CARVER (1864-1943)

Born in slavery, this scientist and teacher earned international respect from his study of agriculture and chemistry, his work with polio sufferers, and helping people of different races to get along.

WINSTON CHURCHILL (1874-1965)

He was the heroic prime minister of Great Britain during World War II, telling his people: "We shall not flag or fail. . . . We shall fight in the fields and in the streets, we shall fight in the hills; we shall never surrender." And they never did.

JACQUES-YVES COUSTEAU (1910-1997)

This French oceanographer, author, and maker of motion pictures about the sea helped to invent the Aqua-Lung, which let divers breathe and swim underwater so they could explore freely. In his boat, *Calypso*, he studied and taught about the world of the sea.

HENRY FORD (1863-1947)

Henry Ford's inexpensive Model T automobile, manufactured on an assembly line (many workers each did a different part of the job, over and over) changed the world forever: *VROOM!*

ANNE FRANK (1929-1945)

Anne was a girl who kept a diary. Thousands of people have read the thoughts and ideas she wrote during the three years she and her family were hiding—just because they were Jews—from the Gestapo (Nazi police) in Amsterdam. She was only one of the millions who died in the Holocaust.

MOHANDAS GANDHI (1869-1948)

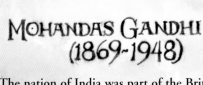

The nation of India was part of the British Empire until Gandhi led his people, without violence, to independence. He was called Mahatma (Great Soul) because of his search for truth and his overcoming of fear. An assassin ended his time on earth.

ADOLF HITLER (1889-1945)

World War I left Germany poor and ruined: a perfect place for people to shout about whose fault it was. Adolf became their leader and promised to win back the empire's glory—besides, he and his Nazi followers thought they knew whom to blame. So 6 million Jewish people were killed. Millions of other people died too, in the crazy wickedness of World War II, set in motion by Adolf Hitler.

MARTIN LUTHER KING, JR. (1929-1968)

He wore many hats: preacher, pastor, writer, and leader of the movement for the civil rights of black Americans. His nonviolent protests were inspired by the work of Mahatma Gandhi in India. They led to the Nobel Peace Prize, the Civil Rights Act of 1964, and Dr. King's assassination, on April 4, 1968.

VLADIMIR ILYICH LENIN (1870-1924)

Lenin, leader of the Communist Bolsheviks became the leader of the Russian Revolution in 1917.

GOLDA MEIR (1898-1978)

She was born in Kiev, Ukraine, and became prime minister of the nation she helped to create. She became known as the Mother of Israel.

ELVIS PRESLEY (1935-1977)

Elvis combined all kinds of music that white and black people liked. His kind of music helped break down some walls in America's divided society. It gave other musicians—and lots of teenagers—lots of ideas. Elvis "the Pelvis" is still known as the King of Rock and Roll.

ELEANOR ROOSEVELT (1884-1962)

Theodore's shy niece married Franklin in 1906. She became an author and speaker for the well-being of all people. Mrs. Roosevelt visited U.S. soldiers overseas, and was a delegate to the United Nations, still working for human rights.

FRANKLIN ROOSEVELT (1882-1945)

When FDR talked on the radio to encourage Americans living in depression hard times or the hard World War II times, many citizens did not even know that their bold, colorful president with the confident smile had long been paralyzed by polio. They did know that he and the government would do just about anything to help "the forgotten man."

THEODORE ROOSEVELT (1858-1919)

T. R., the twenty-sixth president, rancher, hunter, explorer, writer, eager soldier, naturalist, father of six children, and winner of the Nobel Peace Prize, led the United States into a twentieth century of American dominance on the world stage.

CARL SAGAN (1934-1997)

This author and astronomer brought to his home planet a passion for interplanetary exploration out in the cosmic ocean of stars.

DR. JONAS SALK (1914-1995)

He was a scientist who studied how to keep people from getting sick in epidemics. For instance, 20 million people died when they caught influenza, the "flu," in 1918. Ever since ancient times, people were scared of paralyzing polio epidemics—until Dr. Salk tested his polio vaccine on 1.83 million schoolchildren in 1954. It worked!

MARGARET SANGER (1883-1966)

When Margaret Sanger was a young nurse, she saw many women, even her own mother, die at a young age from having too many babies. So she studied and taught about birth control. She had to be tough and brave to do this in the early twentieth century: It was against the law.

KAISER WILHELM II (1859-1959)

Queen Victoria's troublesome grandson, the last emperor of Germany, wanted his country to have more trade, colonies, and battleships than the other European powers. This greedy nationalism led to World War I, then to World War II.

ORVILLE (1878-1948) THE WRIGHT BROTHERS WILBUR (1867-1912)

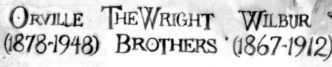

They studied and tinkered with flying ideas in their bicycle shop in Dayton, Ohio, "purely for the pleasure of it," said Wilbur.

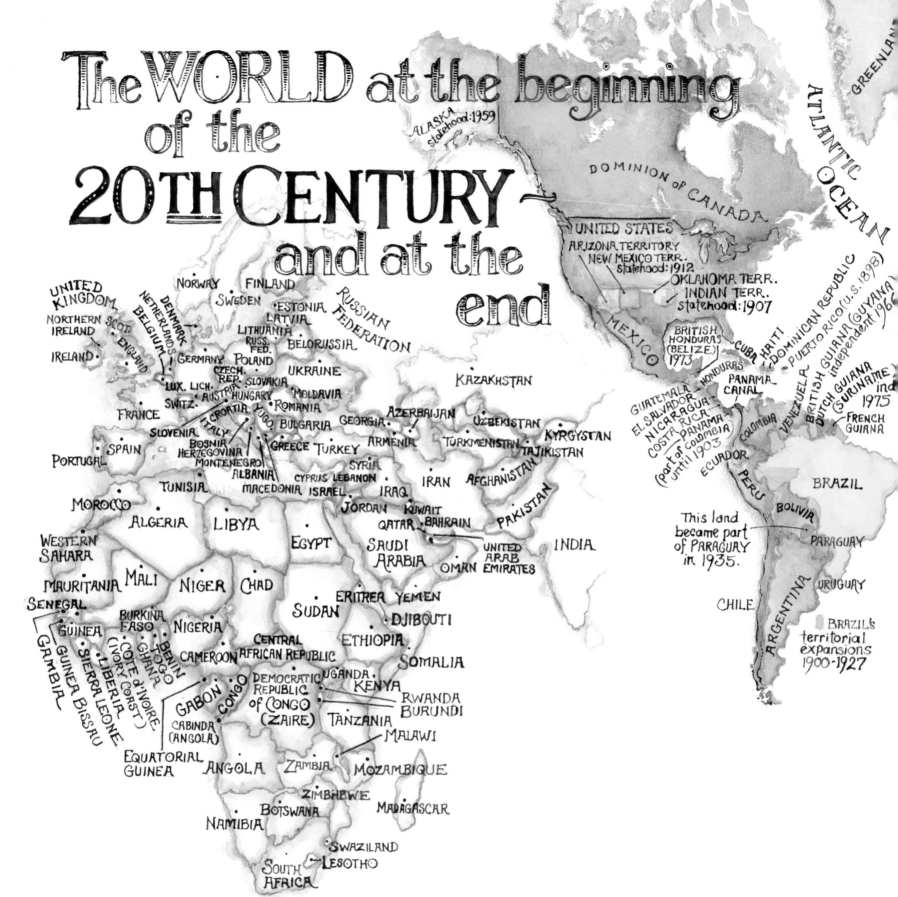

EUROPE BEFORE THE FIRST GREAT WAR

NOVAYA ZEMLYA

ICELAND
NORWAY
SWEDEN
GRAND DUCHY OF FINLAND

SCOTLAND
IRELAND
DENMARK
NETH.
ENGLAND
BELG.
GERMANY
POLAND
FRANCE
SWITZ.
AUSTRIA-HUNGARY
THE UKRAINE
PORTUGAL
SPAIN
ITALY
SERBIA
ROMANIA
BULGARIA
GEORGIA
TUNISIA
GREECE
ALBANIA
MONTENEGRO
CYPRUS
OTTOMAN EMPIRE
PERSIA
AFGHANISTAN

The RUSSIAN empire of the czars lasted 370 years, until the REVOLUTION of 1917 when the communist UNION of SOVIET SOCIALIST REPUBLICS took its place. The USSR lasted until 1991.

MONGOLIA
MANCHURIA

The EMPIRE of CHINA became the communist PEOPLE'S REPUBLIC in 1949.

KOREA

EMPIRE of JAPAN

JAPAN fought CHINA to win control of KOREA and FORMOSA (1894·1895) ~ until 1945

RIO DE ORO
MOROCCO
SPANISH MOROCCO
ALGERIA
LIBYA
EGYPT
ARABIA
OMAN
KUWAIT
BALUCHISTAN
NEPAL
TIBET
BHUTAN
BRITISH INDIAN EMPIRE
INDIA
BURMA (MYANMAR)
FORMOSA (TAIWAN)

HAWAIIAN ISLANDS
U.S. terr. 1898
statehood: 1959

GAMBIA
FRENCH WEST AFRICA
NIGERIA
FRENCH EQUATORIAL AFRICA
KAMERUN
TOGO
GOLD COAST
SIERRA LEONE
LIBERIA
PORTUGUESE GUINEA
RIO MUNI
CABINDA
BELGIAN CONGO
BRITISH EGYPTIAN SUDAN
ERITREA
ADEN
ETHIOPIA
FRENCH
BRITISH
ITALIAN SOMALIA
BRITISH EAST AFRICA
GERMAN EAST AFRICA

PACIFIC OCEAN

FRENCH INDOCHINA (VIET-NAM)
SIAM (THAILAND) 1939
CEYLON (SRI LANKA) 1972
PHILIPPINE ISLANDS (U.S. 1899)
MALAYA
SARAWAK
SUMATRA
BORNEO
CELEBES
NEW GUINEA
NETH. GER. BRIT.

INDIAN OCEAN

DUTCH (NETHERLANDS) EAST INDIES (INDONESIA, 1949)
JAVA

EUROPEAN COLONIAL RULE IN AFRICA IN THE EARLY PART OF THE 20TH CENTURY

ANGOLA
RHODESIA
GERMAN S.W. AFRICA
BECHUANALAND
PORTUGUESE EAST AFRICA
MADAGASCAR
TRANSVAAL
ORANGE FREE STATE
CAPE COLONY
NATAL

FIJI
NEW CALEDONIA
COMMONWEALTH OF AUSTRALIA
TASMANIA
NEW ZEALAND

Legend:
- BELGIAN
- BRITISH
- FRENCH
- GERMAN
- ITALIAN
- PORTUGUESE
- SPANISH
- INDEPENDENT

BIBLIOGRAPHY

DK World Atlas. London: Dorling Kindersley Ltd., 1997.
Grun, Bernard. *The Timetables of History.* New York: Simon & Schuster, 1982.
McCullough, David. *Truman.* New York: Simon & Schuster, 1992.
McEvedy, Colin. *The World History Factfinder.* New York: Gallery Books, 1989.
The World Book Encyclopedia. World Book, Inc., 1985.